Bantam Skylark Books in the Choose Your Own
   Adventure® Series
Ask your bookseller for the books you have missed

YOUR VERY OWN ROBOT

R. A. MONTGOMERY

ILLUSTRATED BY PAUL GRANGER

A BANTAM SKYLARK BOOK®
TORONTO · NEW YORK · LONDON · SYDNEY

RL 2, 007-009

YOUR VERY OWN ROBOT
A Bantam Skylark® Book / April 1982

PRINTING HISTORY

Published simultaneously in hardcover and Skylark®
editions April 1982

2nd printing . . . . . . August 1982	4th printing . . . December 1982
3rd printing . . . September 1982	5th printing . . . . May 1983

CHOOSE YOUR OWN ADVENTURE®
is a registered trademark of Bantam Books, Inc.

Original conception of Edward Packard

Skylark Books is a registered trademark of Bantam Books, Inc.
Registered in U.S. Patent and Trademark Office and elsewhere.

Illustrated by Paul Granger

Library of Congress Cataloging in Publication Data
Montgomery, R. A.
Your very own robot.

(Choose your own adventure; 4)
Summary: The reader is asked to make choices which
will determine the fate of a discarded robot.
[1. Robots—Fiction. 2. Literary recreations]
I. Granger, Paul, ill. II. title. III. Series.

PZ7.M7684Yo	[Fic]	81-70918
ISBN 0-553-05019-2		AACR2
ISBN 0-553-15233-5 (pbk.)		

Published simultaneously in the United States and Canada

PRINTED IN THE UNITED STATES OF AMERICA

CW   15 14 13 12 11 10 9 8 7 6

*This book
is dedicated to
Ramsey and Anson*

*A special
thank you to
Fran Manushkin for
her invaluable
help*

READ THIS FIRST!!!

Most books are about other people.

This book is about you—and your robot!

You and your robot can do anything you decide to do. You can fly, you can take your robot to school. You can even swim in ice cream, if you want. And you can give your robot a name.

Do not read this book from the first page through to the last page.

Instead, start at page one and read until you come to your first choice. Decide what you want to do. Then turn to the page shown and see what happens.

When you come to the end of a story, go back and try another choice. Every choice leads to a new adventure.

Have fun with your robot!

Everybody wants a robot. But only a few **1** people get to have one. That's because robots are hard to make—and they also cost a lot of money.

But you are one of the lucky ones who gets to own a robot. Here's how it happens:

Your mom and dad are scientists. They work with robots every day. Sometimes they even build them.

One day, they build a robot that seems to do everything wrong. "I've tried to fix it and I can't," your father says. So he tosses the robot into the garbage can.

"Poor robot!" you say. "Mom and Dad gave up on you too fast. I think I can fix you up. I've seen them build lots of robots."

Turn to page 2.

2   You get out some nails and a hammer.
And you gather nuts and bolts and some
wire. Bang! Twist! You work on your robot
all day long. Soon it starts to look much better. "You look so good, I'm going to give you
a name," you tell it. So you name your robot
_____.

"There's still more work to do," you tell
your robot. "You could use a few coats of
paint. But I'd really like to turn you on now
and see what you can do."

Your robot should work just as well with-
out paint, shouldn't he?

*If you turn your robot on right away,
turn to page 5.*

If you paint him first, turn to page 6.

NAILS

BOLTS

EXTRA FEET

EXTRA FINGERS
AND HANDS

You turn your robot on. CLICK! He **5** stands up! He sure is tall. Your robot flashes red and blue lights, and his eyes shine bright yellow. "BLOOP-DE-BEEP." he says, holding out his arms to you. "BLEEP-DO-DEEP. I'M ALL YOURS."

"Terrific!" you tell him. "Now I'll turn on your computer." BEEP! BUZZ!

"He works!" you shout. "I fixed him." Then you see a dial on the side of your robot. The dial has numbers from 1 to 100. A sign says: *Turn the dial to your age.* So you do.

"BLEEP!" says your robot. "NOW I CAN TAKE YOU ON AN ADVENTURE THAT'S PERFECT FOR YOU."

But you're not sure if you should go on any adventures yet. After all, you have never used a robot by yourself before.

If you switch him off and ask your parents how to work him, turn to page 9.

If you use your robot right away, turn to page 10.

6   You decide to paint your robot first. So you spray him with bright silver paint, until he shines. Now you are ready to turn him on. CLICK! "GLEEP! BEEP!" is the first thing he says. "I AM SO GLAD TO BE ON. PUT ME TO WORK AND SEE WHAT I CAN DO!"

"I sure will," you tell him.

"FIRST I COULD USE A LITTLE MORE PAINT ON MY BACK," he says.

"OK," you say. You spray a *lot* more paint on him.

"MEEP! IT TICKLES!" yells your robot. He laughs so hard that he falls down and rolls around in the mud.

"Oh, no!" you groan. "Now I have to clean you up."

"NOPE, NEEP!" says your robot. "I CAN WORK JUST AS WELL IF I AM DIRTY."

Maybe he can. But he looks *terrible!*

If you wash your robot, turn to page 14.

If you let him stay muddy, turn to page 16.

You ask your mom and dad how to work **9**
your robot. They show you all his special
knobs and buttons. "Have fun!" says your
mother.

"But be careful," warns your father.
"Some of your robot's buttons may not work
right."

Then they drive off to go shopping.

"I think I will press this button that says
SING," you say.

WHOOSH! Your robot starts to steam.
"No, SING!" you yell.

But he is doing it all wrong. Clouds of
steam are rising from him. Is he going to take
off like a rocket? Yes!

Now what do you do? Should you hop on
him? Or should you call the fire department
to rescue him?

If you leap on your robot, turn to page 19.

If you call the fire department,
turn to page 20.

You want to use your robot right away. So you take him out and show him to your friends. "I want you to meet my robot, _____," you tell them. "I fixed him myself!"

"Show us!" they say. You press your robot's JUMP button. Your robot jumps very high.

Turn to page 12.

12   "Now, STOP!" you shout. But your robot keeps jumping.

"Come back!" you yell, chasing him.

Your robot jumps into an ice cream factory. And he keeps jumping, until he lands—in an *enormous* tub of strawberry ice cream!

"GLUMP!" he yells. "I'M NOT PROGRAMMED TO SWIM."

You know how to swim. But that ice cream looks very cold and thick. What if you sink down in it—forever?

If you yell for help, turn to page 22.

If you dive in to save your robot, turn to page 24.

14   You wash the mud off your robot with the garden hose. Soon he is clean and shiny again.

"Now I will try pressing your RUN button," you tell him. So you do—and off he runs.

"Terrific!" you cry, and you turn him off before he can run too far.

"Say, maybe if I let you run fast enough, you could take off, like a plane!" you say. "But, of course, I don't know how to fly a plane. So that might be dangerous."

"Besides, there are lots of things we could **15** do in the yard. We could build a fort together. That would be a lot of fun."

But you keep thinking about flying. Should you try it? Or should you build the fort?

If you decide to build the fort,
turn to page 27.

If you want to see if your robot can fly,
turn to page 29.

16 You let your robot stay muddy. And you take him for a walk in the neighborhood. Soon a crowd gathers around him.

A junk truck drives by. "Say," shouts the junk man. "That's a nice piece of scrap metal." And he grabs your robot and tosses him into his truck.

"STOP!" you call. But the junk man starts to drive off. Luckily, somebody has called the TV station about your robot, and a TV truck is coming down the street.

Should you ask the TV truck to follow the junk truck? Or should you leap into the junk truck right now and rescue your robot by yourself?

If you leap into the junk truck, turn to page 30.

If you ask the TV truck to follow the junk truck, turn to page 54.

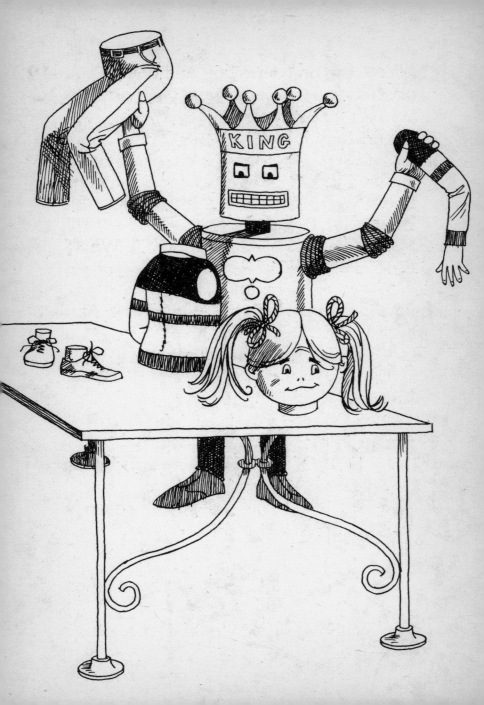

You leap on your robot. And both of you **19**
blast into space. You go past Mars, past Jupiter, past the Milky Way!

You land on Planet Silver, the robot planet. You see thousands of robots, beeping and flashing. "WELCOME!" says the Robot King. "WE ARE GLAD YOU ARE HERE. AND YOU WILL STAY HERE FOREVER BECAUSE WE DON'T WANT EARTH TO KNOW ABOUT US."

"Why not?" you ask.

"BECAUSE THEY WILL MAKE US ALL WORK FOR THEM," says the King.

"I will keep your secret," you say.

"NOPE," says the Robot King. "YOU ARE STAYING WITH US."

Then he takes you apart and builds you into a robot!

"BLEEP! OOPS!" you say. And nobody ever sees you again.

The End

20   You call the fire department to rescue your flying robot. The firemen shoot a huge spray of water at him, and down he comes. "Are you hurt?" you ask, running over to your robot.

"PEEP, NOPE," he says. "BUT I CAN NEVER FLY AGAIN!"

"That's sad," you tell him. "But, of course, you can still do lots of other things."

"NO, NO!" sighs your robot. "I CAN'T. IF I CAN'T FLY I DON'T WANT TO DO ANYTHING."

"That's terrible," you moan.

"THAT'S THE WAY I AM," says your robot. He sits down and clicks off. You try and try, but you can't turn him on again.

"No wonder my parents threw you out," you say. So you get out your hammer and screwdriver and take your robot apart. "I'll build a racing car instead," you say to yourself. You name it _____, the same name as your robot.

The End

"HELP!" you yell.

"ZEEP. ZOOP." your robot says, as he sinks deeper into the strawberry ice cream.

The president of the ice cream factory comes running. He gets you a rubber raft and you jump on it. You row your robot back to safety.

"BLOOP. EEP." he says. "THANKS!"

"That will be $800 for ruining my ice cream," says the president.

"But I don't *have* $800," you say.

"Then you must go to jail," says the president.

"OOP," whispers your robot. "PRESS **23** MY <u>ZIP</u> BUTTON, AND I CAN GET US OUT OF HERE!"

But will he just get you deeper into trouble?

If you press your robot's ZIP button, turn to page 36.

If you decide you'd better go to jail, turn to page 34.

24 You dive into the strawberry ice cream to save your robot. "BRR, it's cold!" you shout. "But it tastes great!" You push your robot to safety.

"We'd better leave before somebody sees us," you tell him.

"OOP! YES!" he says. So you both run out the door and head for home. All your friends laugh when they see you. They even grab spoons and try to scoop off some ice cream.

"Let's take a warm shower," you say to **25**
your robot.

"NO THANKS!" he says. "I'LL RUST."
But he helps scrub your back, and then he
dries you off.

"Next time, try jumping into some *hot
fudge*," you tell him. And both of you laugh.

"You are my best friend," you say to your
robot, and you give him a big hug.

"Now, I'm going to show you my favorite
place of all."

Turn to page 38.

You decide to build a tree fort with your **27** robot. "The maple tree looks best," you say.

"BLEEP!" he agrees.

"Bring me those old boards," you tell him. Slowly, the two of you hammer and saw and build a wonderful fort.

"I can see for miles!" you shout. Just then you see lightning flash, and you hear thunder roar and shake the earth. "Let's get out of here!" you yell.

But before you can climb down the tree, a bolt of lightning comes right at you. Quickly, your robot throws himself in front of you. He saves your life! But the lightning strikes *him*.

"GEEP!" he says, and then he falls to earth and clicks off.

Is he broken forever? Should you try to fix him, or should you wait to see if he wakes up?

If you try to fix him, turn to page 44.

If you wait to see if he wakes up by himself, turn to page 46.

You want to see if your robot can fly. You press his RUN button twice, hoping he will take off like a jet. But instead of flying, your robot leaps into the high telephone wires.

"I'll save you!" you say. You grab a rope and carefully lasso him down.

"WOOPY MOOP!" says your robot. "I DID NOT DO THAT VERY WELL."

"You sure didn't," you say. "I'm never going to press your RUN button again!"

"Now it's time to go to school," you say.

"I'M NOT PROGRAMMED TO GO TO SCHOOL," says your robot. "WHY NOT PRESS MY LASER BUTTON INSTEAD?"

That might be fun! But it could also be dangerous. Maybe you should just take your robot to school.

If you take your robot to school,
turn to page 50.

If you press his laser button,
turn to page 52.

30   "I must save my robot," you yell, as you leap into the junk truck. That makes the junk man very, very angry. "Now, both of you are in serious trouble," he warns.

When he gets to the junkyard, the junk man heads for a huge steam shovel.

"I am going to mash you and your robot to bits!" he screams.

"Get us out of this mess," you tell your robot, pressing his PROBLEM SOLVING button.

"BLEEP! MOOP!" he says. Your robot races the junk man to the steam shovel and gets there first. He scoops up the junk man and drops him onto a huge pile of garbage.

"That's what you get for stealing my robot," you call back to the junk man, as you head home.

"What's for dinner tonight?" you ask your father when you get home.

"Leftovers," he says.

"Ecch. I'll skip it," you say. And you eat potato chips instead.

The End

32   That night, your family watches the news together.

"There you are!" says your mother. "You look terrific."

"We're so proud of you," says your father.

The phone rings just then and you run to get it. "We want to do a story about you and your robot for our newspaper," says a reporter.

"Sure!" you say. And you give your robot another paint job so that *both* of you will look terrific!

The End

34 The president of the ice cream factory takes you and your robot to jail. "BOOP! I DON'T LIKE THIS PLACE," says your robot.

"Neither do I," you moan.

The jailer feeds you bread and water. Your robot gets only oil.

"I wish I never fixed you," you say.

"GLEEP! I WISH YOU HAD LEFT ME IN THE GARBAGE CAN," groans your robot. "AT LEAST THE FOOD WAS GOOD."

You miss your family and your friends a lot. Day after day, you watch old robot shows on TV. "Never try to fix a broken robot," says a scientist.

"*Now* you tell me," you sigh.

One day your mother and father appear on the news. "That's my mother and father," you shout to the jailer.

"Sure, sure," he says. "Make up another good story."

The End

36   You press your robot's ZIP button. Suddenly, your robot starts shooting out paper. "NOW, PRESS MY <u>PRINT</u> BUTTON," he says. So you do. And he starts printing out money! He prints out exactly $800.

"Thanks," says the president of the ice cream factory. "Now, go away."

You run out, very happy. "What a great robot you are," you say. "You are going to print lots of money and make me rich."

"ZOOP! SORRY!" says your robot. "I ONLY PRINT MONEY ONCE EVERY HUNDRED YEARS."

"Why didn't you say that before?" you moan. You are so angry at your robot that you don't talk to him for the rest of the day.

"Well, maybe I will never be rich," you say. "But at least I don't have to go to jail!"

The End

38   You take your robot down to the ocean. "Look at all the ships," you say. "That ship looks very strange. Let's sneak onto it and see what's going on."

"OOP, DEEP!" says your robot, as you climb aboard. "I'M PROGRAMMED TO SOLVE MYSTERIES."

Suddenly, the ship sails off. You are going to sea!

Way out at sea, the crew changes into black clothes. And they put up a new flag—with a skull and crossbones!

"PIRATES!" you yell.

"Stowaways!" shouts the captain. "All **39** stowaways must walk the plank."

The pirates grab you and your robot. You know your robot cannot swim. You can, but there are sharks out there. What should you do?

If you walk the plank, turn to page 40.

If you try to fight the pirates, turn to page 42.

40   "GOOD RIDDANCE," the pirates yell, as they push you off the plank.

SPLASH! BLEEP! You and your robot hit the water. And the ship sails off.

"We're done for," you say.

"DEEPY, FREEP," calls your robot. "IT'S A GOOD THING I'M PROGRAMMED TO CALL WHALES."

"WHOOM!" he calls. And a huge whale leaps up from below.

"ZOOP!" says your robot. "CAN YOU GIVE US A LIFT?"

"WHOOM!" says the whale. And he rides you both back to shore.

"It is time you learned how to swim," you tell your robot. So you spend the rest of the day teaching him.

The End

42 You and your robot are going to fight the pirates. But how? "I will try pressing your SPIN button," you say. It works! Your robot spins so fast that he makes a huge wind. And that huge wind blows all the pirates off the boat!

"Happy landings!" you yell. Then you **43**
radio the Coast Guard to pick up the pirates.

"You get a $5000 reward for finding
them," says the Coast Guard captain. "They
were wanted for smuggling gold."

"TERRIFIC!" you say. Then you turn to
your robot. "I'm sure glad I fished you out of
the garbage can."

"MEEP! ME TOO," says your robot.
"BUT I WISH I HAD A FEW ROBOT
FRIENDS."

So you use the reward money to make a
few more robots. They keep your robot com-
pany when you are at school!

The End

44   "Poor robot," you groan. "I've *got* to bring you back to life."

You pick up your robot and stand him on his funny metal legs. But he wobbles and falls down again—plunk! Then you get an idea.

You run back to the lab as fast as you can, and you look through your parents' special emergency repair kit. You grab one part and bring it back. Carefully you take off your robot's head and put the part right in the middle of his chest.

Your robot's lights start to flash again. His arms and legs jerk, and he stands up!

"CLOSE CALL!" he says. "VERY CLOSE CALL!"

"I'm so glad you're OK," you shout. And you give him the biggest hug you can!

The rain has stopped and the sun is out again. You and your robot climb back up to your fort. And you play there for the rest of the day.

The End

46   Your robot looks like he's waking up. "WOOP!" he says. "THAT LIGHTNING GAVE ME A BURST OF ENERGY! I'M READY TO FLY TO ANOTHER PLANET!" And off he goes! You grab onto his legs just in time, and you fly off with him.

"Let's go to Venus," you say.

"ROGER!" says your robot. And you fly fast through a haze of yellow light.

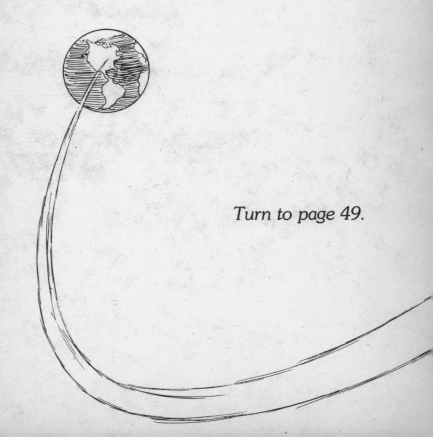

Turn to page 49.

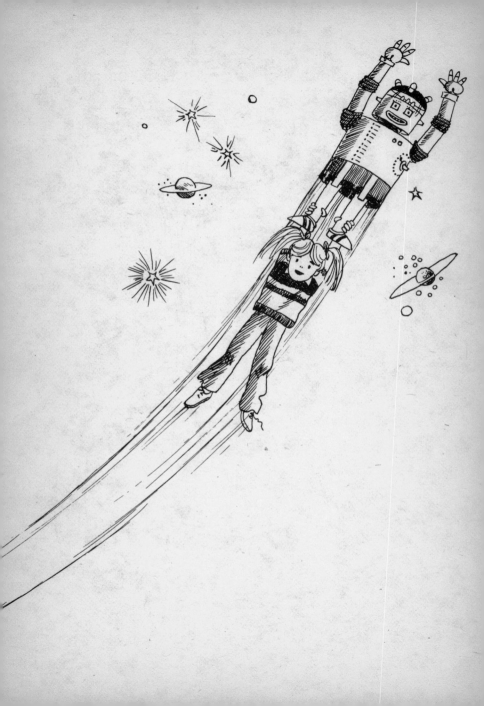

Venus is all soft and yellow and gooey, like half-melted butter. The whole planet is like a huge amusement park!

You play all day, and then you fly home in time for dinner.

"How did your shoes get so sticky?" asks your father.

"I—uh, don't know," you answer.

"I DO!" laughs your robot from under the table. Quickly, you turn him off so he doesn't tell.

And nobody ever knows you really went to Venus!

The End

50 You take your robot to school. Of course, all the kids love him. "Can your robot clean out the wastebasket and pass out the chalk?" asks your teacher, Mr. Sims.

"Sure," you say, though you don't really know for sure. You press a few buttons and turn your robot loose. He picks up the wastebasket and dumps it on your teacher's desk!

"STOP!" you yell. But he doesn't! He takes all the chalk and breaks it and throws it out the window!

Mr. Sims runs up to your robot and yells, "If you do not stop, I am going to make you stay after school and write 'I AM A BAD ROBOT' on the blackboard one thousand times."

"I AM NOT PROGRAMMED FOR THAT!" says your robot, and he runs out the door.

The next day you have to stay after school and write 'I AM A VERY BAD ROBOT TRAINER'—one thousand times!

Phooey!

The End

ZAP! You press the LASER button on your robot. The beam flashes on. But there's one thing wrong—the beam is aimed right at you! You leap up into the air and the beam misses you by an inch. But it burns down the rose bushes in Mr. Grump's garden!

The Grumps are roaring mad! They tell your mom and dad. And you have to spend every day for a week planting new roses.

"SORRY! I AM NOT PROGRAMMED TO PLANT ROSE BUSHES," laughs your robot.

You laugh too—because it *is* very funny!

The End

54 "STOP!" you yell at the TV truck. You tell the cameraman about your robot. "A scoop!" he yells. "We will save your robot *and* show it on TV too!"

So you all drive off after the junk man.

Suddenly, the junk truck comes to a red light. It stops so fast that the TV truck bumps into it. Your robot flies high up into the air!

You run out of the TV truck and look up. PLOP! Your robot drops right into your arms.

"Good shot!" says the TV man. "We will use it on the news tonight."

A policeman comes by and arrests the junk man for "robotnapping."

Turn to page 32.

ABOUT THE AUTHOR

R. A. Montgomery is an educator and publisher. A graduate of Williams College, he also studied in graduate programs at Yale University and New York University. After serving in a variety of administrative capacities at Williston Academy and Columbia University, he co-founded the Waitsfield Summer School in 1965. Following that, Montgomery helped found a research and development firm specializing in the development of educational programs. He worked for several years as a consultant to the Peace Corps in Washington, D.C. and West Africa. For the last seven years, he has been both a writer and a publisher.

ABOUT THE ILLUSTRATOR

Paul Granger is a prize-winning illustrator and painter.

DO YOU LOVE
CHOOSE YOUR OWN ADVENTURE®?
Let your older brothers and sisters in on the fun.

You know how great CHOOSE YOUR OWN AD-VENTURE® books are to read over and over again. But did you know that there are CHOOSE YOUR OWN ADVENTURE® books for older kids too? They're just as much fun as the CHOOSE YOUR OWN AD-VENTURE® books you read and they're filled with the same kinds of decisions—but they're longer and have even more ways for the story to end.

So get your older brothers and sisters and anyone else you know between the ages of nine and thirteen in on the fun by introducing them to the exciting world of CHOOSE YOUR OWN ADVENTURE®.

There are over twenty CHOOSE YOUR OWN AD-VENTURE® books for older kids now available wherever Bantam paperbacks are sold.

AV9—4/83